W9-BBO-693

and the Greatest Trick Ever!

For Michael Hans—P.J.

For A.J. Paxton, who could probably figure
out how to make a cat disappear!—M.J.

Text copyright © 2002 by Pamela Jane
Illustrations copyright © 2002 by Meredith Johnson
under exclusive license to MONDO Publishing

All rights reserved.
No part of this publication may be reproduced, except in the case of quotation
for articles or reviews, or stored in any retrieval system, or transmitted in any
form or by any means, electronic, mechanical, photocopying, recording, or
otherwise, without written permission from the publisher.

For information contact:
MONDO Publishing
980 Avenue of the Americas
New York, NY 10018
Visit our website at www.mondopub.com
Printed in China
06 07 08 09 HC 10 9 8 7 6 5 4 3 2 1
10 11 12 13 14 PB 10 9 8 7 6 5

First published in paperback in 2004

ISBN 1-59034-187-2 (hardcover)   ISBN 1-59034-184-8 (pbk.)

Designed by Edward Miller

Library of Congress Cataloging-in-Publication Data

Jane, Pamela.
    Milo and the greatest trick ever! / by Pamela Jane ; illustrated by Meredith Johnson.
        p. cm.
    Summary: For his performance at the neighborhood show, Milo makes Rainbow the cat
disappear but then has trouble finding her afterwards.
    ISBN 1-59034-187-2 (hc.) -- ISBN 1-59034-184-8 (pbk.)
    [1. Magic tricks--Fiction. 2. Cats--Fiction. 3. Talent shows--Fiction.] I. Johnson,
Meredith, ill. II.Title.

PZ7 .J213 Mk 2002
[E]--dc21   2002067050

Milo

and the Greatest Trick Ever!

by Pamela Jane

Illustrated by Meredith Johnson

Milo and his friend Annie wanted to put on a show. They were going to surprise the neighborhood kids with their best tricks.

"Just wait until everyone sees my trick!"
said Milo. "It's the greatest trick ever!"
"What are you going to do?" asked Annie.

"I'm going to make Rainbow go
POOF!" said Milo. "Now you see her . . . now
you don't!"

Rainbow was a stray cat. All of the kids
in the neighborhood helped take care of her.

6

Milo always left a bowl of milk under the porch for Rainbow.

"I'll hold a big red sheet in front of
Rainbow," said Milo. "She'll run under the
porch. When I move the sheet—*POOF!*
Rainbow will be gone!"

"How will you get her to come back?"
asked Annie.

Milo grinned. "That's where you
can help."

"You will be hiding under the porch.
When it's time for Rainbow to come back,
you will chase her out!" said Milo.

At last it was the day of the show. All
the kids on the block came to watch.
"Let the show begin!" shouted Milo.

First Annie stood on her head.

"That's easy!" said Milo's big sister,
Sam. "Anyone can do that."

Next Milo walked on his hands. No one else could do that. All the kids cheered.

Then Annie wiggled her ears and moved her eyebrows at the same time. Jason yawned loudly.

Milo jumped up.

"Watch, everyone!" he shouted. "I will now show you the greatest trick ever!"

Milo set Rainbow next to the porch. He
waved a big red sheet in front of her.
"One, two, three!" he counted.

Milo dropped the sheet.

POOF!

"Wow!" yelled Luke. "Rainbow's gone!"

"Now for the good part!" said Milo.

He waved the sheet again.

"Three, two, one . . . watch the fun!"

Milo pulled the sheet back.

"Ta-dah!" he cried.

No one said a word.

Milo looked behind the sheet. Rainbow was not there.

"Where's Rainbow?" Milo whispered
to Annie.

"I don't know!" Annie whispered back.
"It's your trick."

"Bring Rainbow back! Bring Rainbow
back!" all the kids shouted.

Milo's face turned red.

"Uh . . . you'll have to come back
tomorrow to see the end of the trick!"

"What are we going to do?" Milo asked
Annie after the kids went home. "I don't
know how to bring Rainbow back!"

"So much for the greatest trick ever,"
said Sam.

"Maybe Wolf can find her," said Milo. "Where's Rainbow, Wolf?"

Wolf put his nose to the ground and took off running. Milo and Annie ran after him.

Wolf followed his nose straight to Mrs.
Mackey's garbage can. Wolf tipped over
the can and found lots of garbage—but
no Rainbow.

Milo put a bowl of milk and the red
sheet under the porch before he went
to bed that night.

The next morning, Milo heard kids
out in the yard.

"Milo! Come outside quick!"
Annie shouted.

Milo went out to the front porch to see
what was going on. He couldn't believe
his eyes!

"How did you do that, Milo?" asked
Brad. "Yesterday there was one cat. Today
there are seven!"

"Wow!" said Luke. "Now that's
a great trick."

"Yeah!" Annie said. "The greatest
trick ever!"